# Richard Scarry's
# BEST STORY BOOK
# EVER

This book contains a selected sampling of stories, rhymes,
and pictures from Richard Scarry's favorite Golden Books.
The subject matter covers a wide field and includes Words,
Numbers, Alphabets, Fables, Manners, Safety Rules,
Adventure Stories, Mother Goose Rhymes, Colors,
a Calendar Story, a Christmas Story, Cars, Trucks, Planes,
Trains, Boats, lots of Nonsense, and hundreds of Animals,
all presented in an entertaining and informative manner.

*All the stories are by Richard Scarry unless otherwise indicated.*

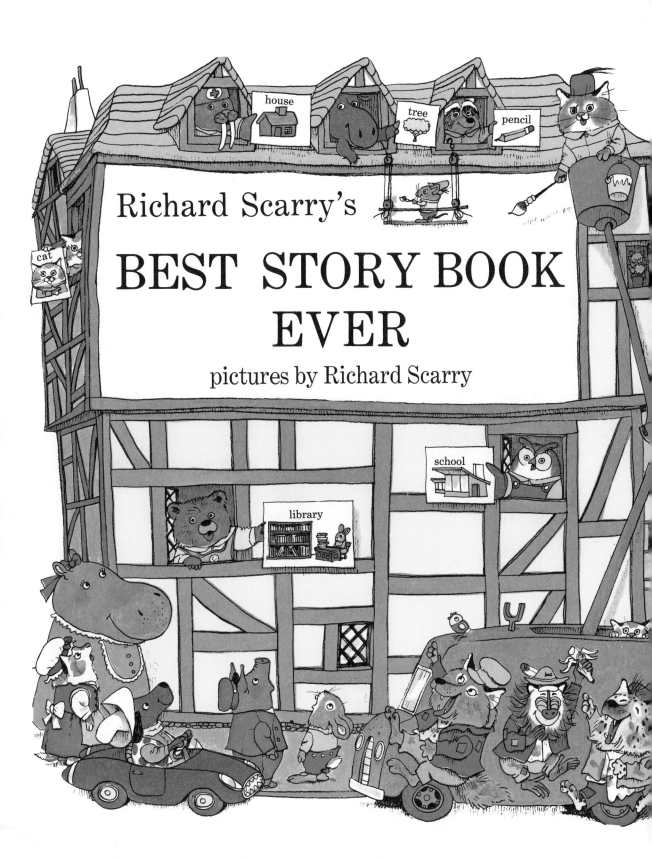

# Richard Scarry's
# BEST STORY BOOK EVER

pictures by Richard Scarry

**A GOLDEN BOOK · NEW YORK**

Golden Books Publishing Company, Inc.,
New York, New York 10106

# Contents

© 1968 Golden Books Publishing Company, Inc. *Richard Scarry's Storybook Dictionary*
Copyright © 1966 by Richard Scarry. Copyright renewed 1994 by Patricia Scarry
and Richard Scarry II. *My Golden Go-Go Library: Planes, Cars, Trains, Boats*
Copyright © 1967 by Richard Scarry. Copyright renewed 1995 by Patricia Scarry and
Richard Scarry II. All rights reserved. Printed in the U.S.A. No part of this book may
be reproduced or copied in any form without written permission from the publisher.
All trademarks are the property of Golden Books Publishing Company, Inc.

Library of Congress Catalog Card Number: 68-28867

ISBN: 0-307-16548-5

MM

window     curtains

# THE NEW DAY

It is the morning of a new day.
The sun is shining.
Little Bear gets up out of bed.

face cloth

soap

towel

toothbrush

toothpaste

comb

pajamas

First he washes
his face and hands.

Then he brushes
his teeth.

He combs
his hair.

shirt

pants

He dresses
himself.

He makes
his bed.

He comes promptly when
he is called to breakfast.

Bear sits up straight
in his chair.

He is very hungry.
This is what he eats.

cold fruit juice

warm cereal

with cream

pancakes

with butter and maple syrup

He doesn't eat
the toaster.

fried eggs

bacon

toast

honey

jam

hot cocoa

cool milk

and a waffle.

When he finishes eating breakfast he helps
his mother to wash and dry the dishes.

cup

saucer

plate

bowl

fork

knife

spoon

glass

jar

pitcher

frying pan

lid

pot

pan

bottle

juice squeezer

Now he is ready to play with his friends.

# THE RABBIT FAMILY'S HOUSE

Father Rabbit, Mother Rabbit,
and the Rabbit Brothers
are getting ready for the new day.
Their friend Owl is waiting
for the two brothers to come out
to play. Can you find him?

chimney

roof

father

mirror

lamp

bed

bedroom

cupboard

dining
room

kitchen

table

sink

back door

chair

floor

stove

mother

woodpile

lawn

bird bath

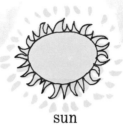

sun

WHOO   owl

smoke   antenna

light switch

television set

record player

hassock

bunk bed

bathroom

upstairs hall

boys' bedroom

front door

living room

picture   candle

outside light

telephone   fireplace

stairs

sofa or couch

front hall

lamp

door mat

rug

stone walk   window

# FEED BIG HILDA HIPPO HER ABC'S

Charlie Chipmunk has invited Big Hilda Hippo to dinner. But Charlie can't decide what to feed her. Will you help Charlie pick the proper ABC food to feed Big Hilda?

# Aa

Would you feed her an **automobile**?
Or an **apple**?
Which would you feed her?

# Bb

Would a **bed** be good to eat?
Or a **banana**?

Did you ever see a hippo eat a **bed**?

10

# Cc

Would she like to eat
a **clock**?
Or a **carrot**?

If she ate a **clock**
she might always say "Tick-tock."

# Dd

Would you serve her
a **doughnut**
with a hole?

Or a **drum**?

Do you eat a **drum** with a fork
or with a spoon?

# Ee

Do you think
she would
like an **egg**?
Or an **engine**?

Which would you prefer?

# Ff

Is a **fan** good to eat?
Or **fudge**?

# Gg

Would you give her **grapes**?
Or a **glove**?

If she ate one **glove** do you think
she should eat another so that
she would have a pair?

# Hh

Would she like to eat a **hat**?
Or a **hot dog**?

Do you put mustard
on the **hats** you eat?

# Ii

I know she would like some **ice cream**.     Wouldn't you?

# Jj

Do you think she would
like a juicy **jeep**?
Or **jam**?

What does a **jeep** taste like?
Does it taste like **jam**?

# Kk

How would Hilda like a nice
ripe **kite**?

Or do you think a candy **kiss** is nicer?

# Ll

Is Hilda hungry enough to
    eat all this **laundry**?

Maybe she would like
    some **lemonade** instead.

# Mm

Shall we feed her
    a **mop**?

Or a great big slice of **melon**?

# Nn

Do you think she would like
    to chew on a **nest**?

Or would she rather
    have a **nut**?

# Oo

Shall we feed her some nice fresh **overalls**?

Or an **orange**?

# Pp

How about a nice **piano** to munch on?

Or a **peach**?

A **piano** is a lot more to eat than a **peach**. Wouldn't you rather eat a **piano**?

# Qq

Do you eat a **quilt** while sitting up or lying down?

I don't think Hilda wants to eat a **quilt**.

15

# Rr

Is Hilda hungry enough to eat a **refrigerator**?
Or would she prefer a **roast** of beef?

# Ss

Now, shall we give her a
**sandwich** with salt on it?
Or a **stove** with pepper on it?

# Tt

Termites are little insects who like to eat **tables** and anything else made of wood. Would Hilda like to eat a **table** or a **tomato**?

Wow! Look at that termite eat that **table**!

# Uu

Anyone who would try to eat an **umbrella** would be very silly. Please don't feed an **umbrella** to Hilda. It tastes awful.

# V v
Instead, feed Hilda her **vitamins**.

# W w
She will need a glass of **water** to wash them down.

# X x
Hilda has finished her dinner.
She puts her knife and fork on her plate.
They look like the letter **X**.

# Y y
She opens her mouth wide and **yawns**.

# Zz

She is sleepy after such a big meal.
Off to sleep she goes. ZZZzzzzzzzzzzzzzzz!

Hilda wants to thank you and Charlie for feeding her.
This is what she ate.

And if you are hungry tonight before
   you go to bed—eat something!
But . . . never, never, never
   eat your bed!

# TOYS

tricycle

Toys and games have names, too.
When you play with toys,
it is more fun if you
share them with your friends.
When you play games you may win
and sometimes you may lose.
Bear is a good sport. He is
losing a game but he might
win the next time. Do you think
he might win the next game?

doll

blocks

teddy bear

rocking horse

Bear is losing.

game

Rabbit is winning.

20

castle

croquet

toy soldiers

tea set

robot

racing car

typewriter

bean bags

doll house

scooter

glider

bow and arrow

# WORDS TO LEARN

## PARTS OF THE BODY

Everyone has a **body.**
Every **body** has many
different parts to it.
We use words to name parts
of the **body.** Ali Cat and
Squeaky have drawn pictures
which show us the different
parts. Some of us have tails.
What kind of tail do you have?

THE HEAD

hair
eye
ear
cheek
nose
tongue
face
tooth
lips
chin

THE BODY

head
wrist
neck
shoulder
arm
elbow
chest
paw or hand
stomach
waist
knee
claw or finger
foot
tail
leg
claw or toe
heel
ankle

mouth
teeth

TAILS

# THE FAMILY

Grandma

Mother

Sister Kitty

Uncle Louie

Father Cat

Babykins

Brother Tom

Aunty and
all the cousins

Uncle and Aunty Cat and their children
visit the Cat **family**. Uncle Louie is
Mother Cat's brother. All belong
to the same **family**.

| January February March | April May June | July August September | October November December |
|---|---|---|---|

# THE MONTHS OF THE YEAR

There are four seasons in the year.
They are spring, summer,
fall, and winter.

Sunday
Monday
Tuesday
Wednesday
Thursday
Friday
Saturday

# THE DAYS OF THE WEEK

Ali Cat is teaching Squeaky
about **days**. A **day** is one
**daytime** and one nighttime.
A **day** has a morning, a noon,
an afternoon, an evening,
and a night. There are seven
**days** in a week. Can you
write them, Squeaky?
Very good, Squeaky.

# Mother Goose Rhymes

With letters we can make words.
With words we can make rhymes
and stories.
Let us read some Mother Goose
rhymes.

Old Mother Goose,
When she wanted to wander,
Would ride through the air
On a very fine gander.

Tom, Tom, the piper's son,
Stole a pig and away did run.
The pig was eat, and Tom
was beat,
And Tom went crying
down the street.

GINGERBREAD PIGS

This little pig went to market,

This little pig stayed at home,

This little pig had roast beef,

This little pig had none,

And this little pig cried, Wee-wee-wee-wee-wee,
I can't find my way home.

Now let us read some stories.

# THE FISHING CAT

### by Patricia Scarry

A cat went down to the sea to fish.
He wanted to catch a whale.

Did he catch a big, big whale?

No!
He caught
a big, big log.

Did he toss the log back into the sea?

No. The cat did not.
He took out his knife and he cut the log.
He cut it here and there.
Now why did the cat do that?

He did it to make a fine fishing boat.

So LOOK OUT all you whales!

# I AM A BUNNY

*by Ole Risom*

I am a bunny.
My name is Nicholas.
I live in a hollow tree.

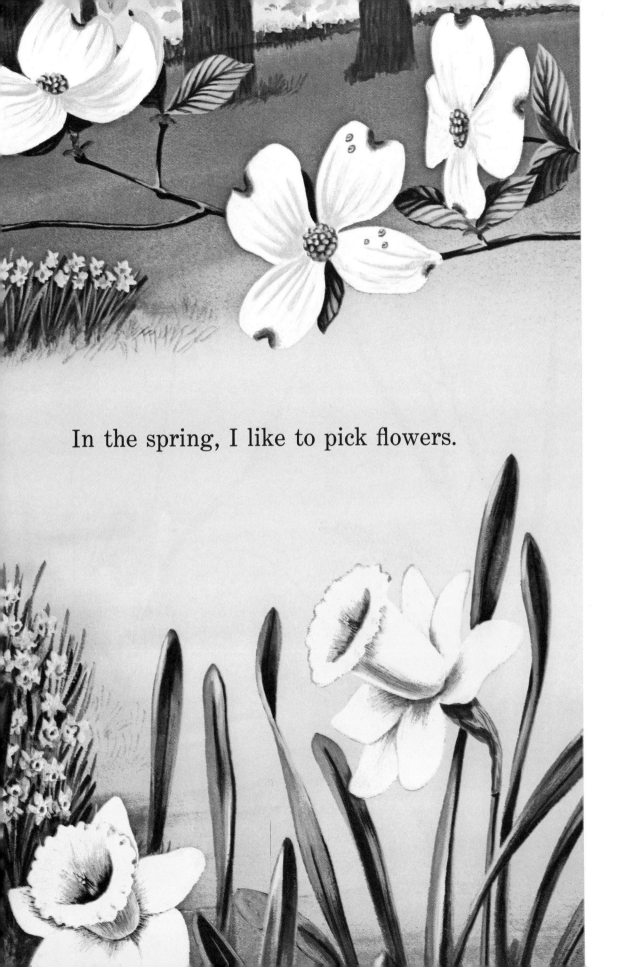

In the spring, I like to pick flowers.

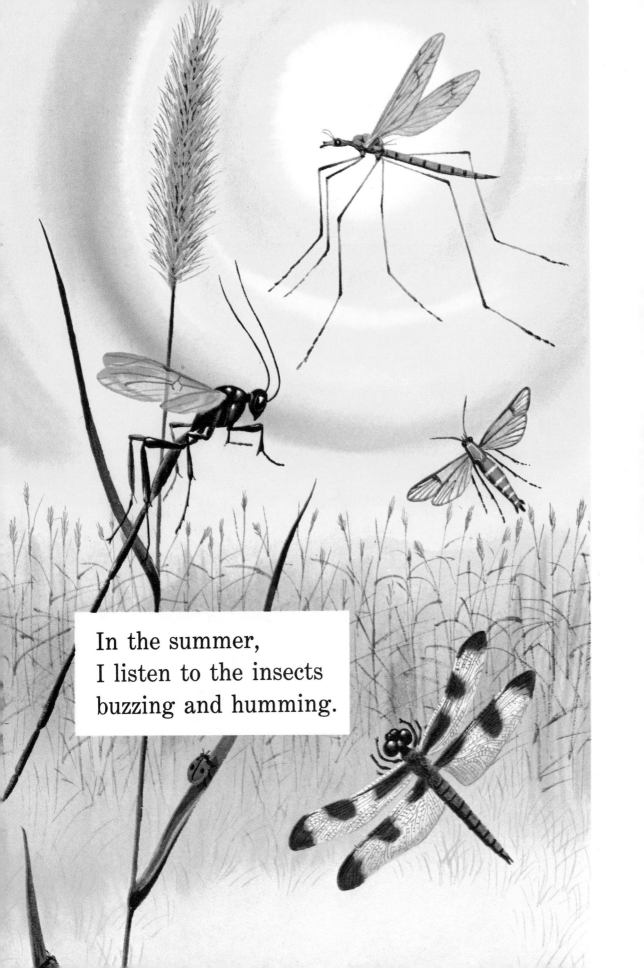

In the summer,
I listen to the insects
buzzing and humming.

In the fall,
I like to watch the leaves
falling from the trees.

And, when winter comes,
I watch the snow falling from the sky.

Then I curl up in my hollow tree
and dream about spring.

# Good Night, Little Bear

*by Patricia Scarry*

It is time for Little Bear to go to bed.
Mother Bear closes the storybook.
She gives Little Bear a good-night kiss.

Then over to
his big furry father
runs the little bear.

Wheee!

Father Bear swings his little one high up
to his shoulders for a ride to bed.

"Duck your head," calls Mother Bear, just in time. And into the snug little bedroom they go.

Squeak!
The tiny bed sighs as Father Bear sits down.
"Now, into bed with you," he says.
He waits for Little Bear to climb down.
But Little Bear doesn't move.
He sits up on his father's shoulders and grins.
Father Bear waits. He yawns a rumbly yawn.
Is Father Bear falling asleep?
No. Suddenly he opens his eyes again.

"Why, I must have been dreaming,"
says Father Bear, pretending to wake up.
But what's this?
There is no furry head on the pillow.
Where can Little Bear be?
Father Bear looks under the pillow.
Nobody there.
He doesn't seem to feel
something tickling his ear.

Aha.
There's a lump down under the blanket.
Father Bear pats the lump.
But it doesn't squeak or wiggle.
Can it be Little Bear?

Why, it's the toy teddy and the blue bunny
waiting for Little Bear to come to bed!

"Mother, that naughty bear is hiding,"
says Father Bear to Mother Bear, with a wink.
"Maybe he's hiding under the kitchen stove,"
says Mother Bear, who loves a joke.

Bang! Bang!
Father Bear rattles the pots and pans
on top of the stove.
"Little Bear, I'm coming to get you!" he roars.

Father Bear reaches under the stove.
He feels something soft and furry.
Is it Little Bear?

No.
It's only Father Bear's old winter mitten.

'Way up high Little Bear claps his paw
to his mouth. But not in time.
"I heard that Little Bear laugh," says Father.
"Now where can he be hiding?

"Is he standing outside the front door?
I'll turn the knob softly –
and fling the door wide!"
No. There are no bears out there.
Just a family of fat little rabbits
nibbling lettuce in the garden.
"Shoo!" snorts Father Bear.

"Something is hiding in the woodbox,"
whispers Mother Bear.
"Creep over there on tip toe,
and you may catch a little bear."
Eeek!
There's just a wee mouse hiding there.

There's nobody up high, on the china shelf.
"Ouch!"
Little Bear bumps his head.
"Who said Ouch?" asks Father Bear.
"Mother, did you say Ouch?"
"Not I," smiles Mother Bear.
Oh she is a tease.

"Now where is that naughty bear hiding?
He wouldn't run away.
Not a little bear who is always hungry
for chocolate cake."
And that big Daddy Bear cuts himself a huge piece
of chocolate cake right under the little bear's nose.

Little Bear suddenly feels hungry.
But just then Father Bear stops smack
in front of the mirror.
"Why, there he is," roars the big bear.
"But you couldn't find me," squeaks Little Bear,
reaching for the chocolate cake.

Wheee!
Off Daddy's shoulders and down to the sofa.
Bounce. Bounce. Bounce.
"Wasn't that a good hiding place, Mommy?
No one could find me up there."

"But I've found you now," says Father Bear.
Little Bear wiggles and giggles under his Daddy's
strong arm . . . all the way into bed.

"Did I really fool you, Daddy?"
asks Little Bear.
Father Bear just laughs and winks.

Do you think Father Bear knew all the time?

# WORK MACHINES

Busy, busy, busy bears.
Most of the bears are busy
moving dirt with their machines.

bulldozer

shovel

dump trailer

But there is one bear
who has a machine which
does something else to the dirt.
Which one is it? What is he doing?

tractor scraper

tractor shovel

bucket loader

dump truck

dirt

roller

smooth dirt

and tractor

rough dirt

# ANIMALS

All **animals** move about.

bee

mouse

monkey

Some **animals** hop, jump, and run.

kangaroo

pig

otter

grasshopper

crocodile

Some **animals** have tails.

cat

tiger

squirrel

ant

anteater

Some **animals** have big noses.

elephant

crab

turtle

mouse

Some have shells.

warthog

Some **animals** are beautiful.

Dingo Dog

Some drive too fast.

swordfish

tunafish

not really?

no fooling!

shark

Some **animals** tell stories.

pig

lion

walrus

Some eat too much.

Some help other **animals**
get well when they are sick.

heron

stork

rooster

hen and
chickens

penguin

cat

pig

All **animals** love
to read books.

Some **animals** hate to take baths.

The pretty colored birds like
to have their picture taken.
Watch the birdie, birds!

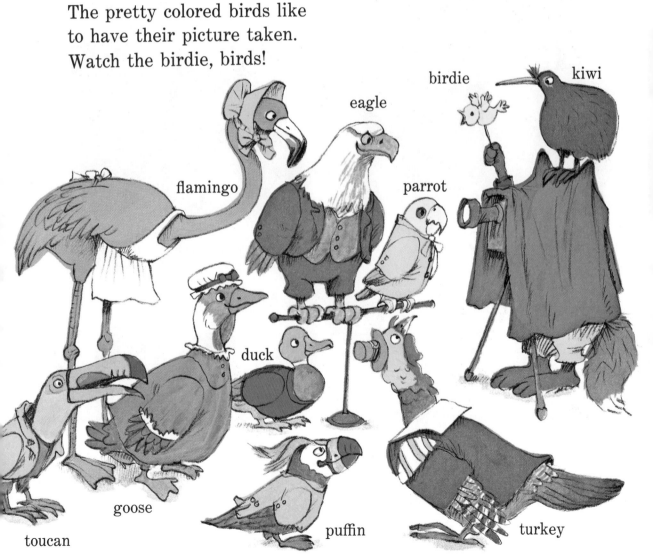

birdie

kiwi

eagle

flamingo

parrot

duck

goose

toucan

puffin

turkey

chamois

gnu

reindeer

antelope

kudu

musk ox

Some **animals** have horns.

yak

bighorn
sheep

68

Some **animals** are insects and bugs.

Some bugs dive.
Some insects wear four shoes.

praying mantis

cricket

beetle

bear

Some **animals** wear coats
that are too big for them.

tiger

Some **animals** wiggle and
crawl and spell words.

Some are not very
good fishermen.

octopus

pig

Some **animals** can
reach all the
way across the
table, My, what
bad manners!

Spuds Bug

worm

Some **animals** live in houses.

snake

At least one sleeps with his shoe on.

frog

The frogs are lucky to have a swimming pool.

bass fiddle

triangle

trumpet

cymbals

Some **animals** make very fine music.
Toot toot!
Boom boom!
Twang twang!

THE CATS' MEOWERS

piano

drum

cat

goat

owl

mouse

moose

canoe

Some ride in boats.

Baron von Crow

Some **animals** ride on trains . . .

baboon

wolf

. . . while others
ride bicycles.

laughing hyena

owl

bird

Some **animals** fly.

Some insects fly.

skunk

All flies fly.
Close the door please!

raccoon

rabbit

leopard

Paper airplanes fly.
Some **animals**
are naughty.

Mr. Fixit Fox wears
rubber boots to keep
his feet dry.

leaking pipe

Grandma sews Tom Cat's pants
to keep his seat warm.

# SHAPES

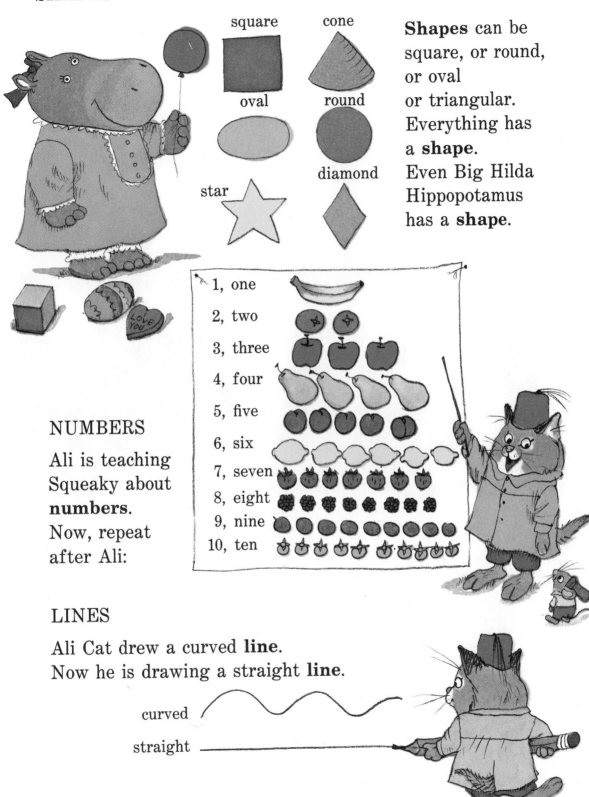

square

cone

oval

round

star

diamond

**Shapes** can be square, or round, or oval or triangular. Everything has a **shape**. Even Big Hilda Hippopotamus has a **shape**.

1, one
2, two
3, three
4, four
5, five
6, six
7, seven
8, eight
9, nine
10, ten

## NUMBERS

Ali is teaching Squeaky about **numbers**. Now, repeat after Ali:

## LINES

Ali Cat drew a curved **line**.
Now he is drawing a straight **line**.

curved

straight

# Farmer Pig

FARMER PIG PLANTED
A SEED OF CORN
IN THE GROUND.

THE RAIN CAME DOWN
AND WET THE SEED
THE SEED
STARTED TO GROW.

THE SUN
SHONE DOWN,
AND WARMED
THE SEED.
SOON,
LITTLE LEAVES
SPROUTED UP
FROM THE GROUND.

IT GREW AND GREW
FINALLY,
IT HAD THREE EARS OF CORN,
READY TO BE PICKED.

FARMER PIG GAVE
ONE EAR TO MR. CROW.

HE GAVE ONE EAR TO HIS WIFE.
SHE LOVED CORN!

AND WITH HIS KNIFE,
FARMER PIG MADE
THE THIRD EAR
INTO A PIPE!
ISN'T IT WONDERFUL
TO THINK OF WHAT
YOU CAN DO WITH
ONE LITTLE SEED!

brook

meadow

haystacks

apple orchard

corn field

plowed field

lane

fence

stone wall

vegetable garden

gate

barn

barnyard

hayloft

water pump

farmhouse

# ON THE FARM

Farmer Hee Haw is
working on his farm.
He is growing vegetables
to sell at the market.
He doesn't have any time
to spend with visitors.

rake

milk can

hoe

ladder

scythe

pail

farm truck

tractor

pitchfork

wagon

Farmer Hee Haw is taking the
vegetables to the market to sell.
My! That is a bumpy road!

corn

peas

celery

asparagus

lettuce

potato

tomatoes

beets

onions

carrots

turnip

cauliflower

cucumbers

beans

pumpkin

cabbage

squash

# MEALTIME

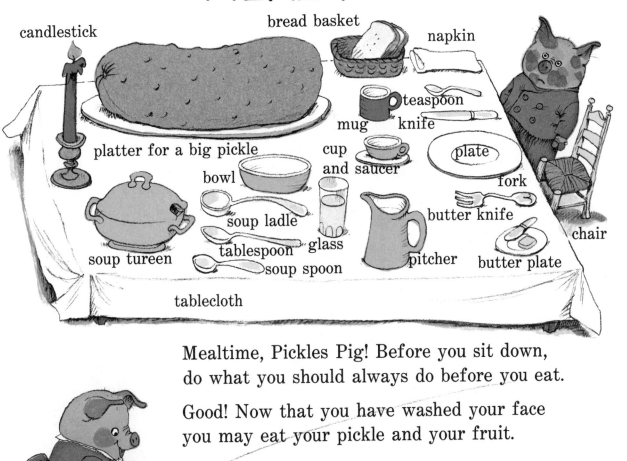

candlestick
bread basket
napkin
teaspoon
mug
knife
platter for a big pickle
cup and saucer
plate
bowl
fork
soup ladle
butter knife
tablespoon
glass
chair
soup tureen
soup spoon
pitcher
butter plate
tablecloth

Mealtime, Pickles Pig! Before you sit down, do what you should always do before you eat.

Good! Now that you have washed your face you may eat your pickle and your fruit.

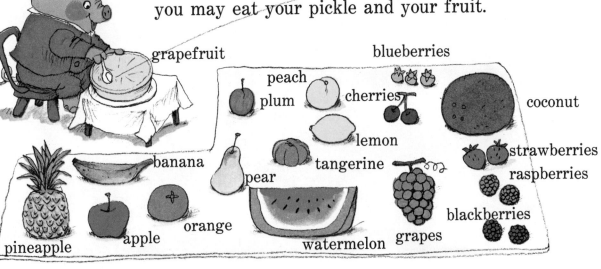

grapefruit
blueberries
peach
plum
cherries
coconut
lemon
banana
tangerine
strawberries
raspberries
pear
blackberries
pineapple
apple
orange
watermelon
grapes

Dear me! Pickles Pig ate too much. He was so sleepy he lay down and took a nap!

# PIP PIP GOES
# TO LONDON

Pip Pip Cat went to London
to seek his fame and fortune
in the service of the Queen.

First, he went to
the Tower of London,
to see if he could be
a Beefeater,
which means a Guardian
of the Queen's jewels.
No! They didn't need
any more guards.

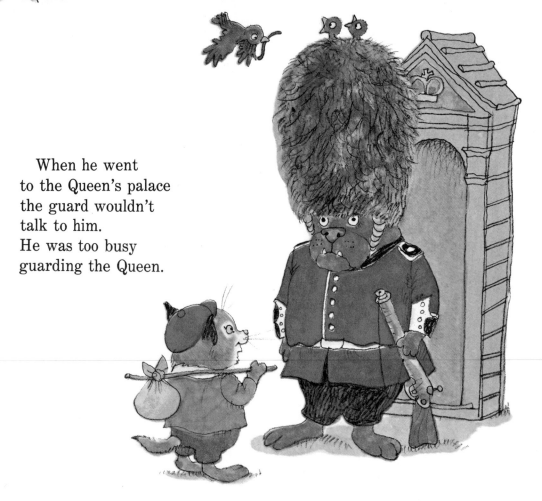

When he went
to the Queen's palace
the guard wouldn't
talk to him.
He was too busy
guarding the Queen.

At the Admiralty, where they guard
the Queen's Navy, he was afraid of
being stepped upon and so he quickly left.

Pip Pip was very sad. He wouldn't be able to serve
the Queen after all. "The Queen must be very sad too,"
he said to himself. "She has lost her ring."

He passed a fountain into
which people had thrown pennies
for good luck. He saw
something which didn't
look like a penny.
It was golden! It glittered!

It was a ring!
Maybe it was the Queen's ring!!
He showed it to a policeman.
They hurried off to see
the Queen. It was the Queen's ring!
She was very happy to have it back.

The Queen made Pip Pip
"The Queen's Guard of
Her Majesty's Fountains."
Every day, he scooped out
the "good luck" pennies.
The Queen used the money
to buy food for the poor
stray cats who had no
homes and lived in alleys.
Wasn't she a nice Queen?

# BUILDINGS

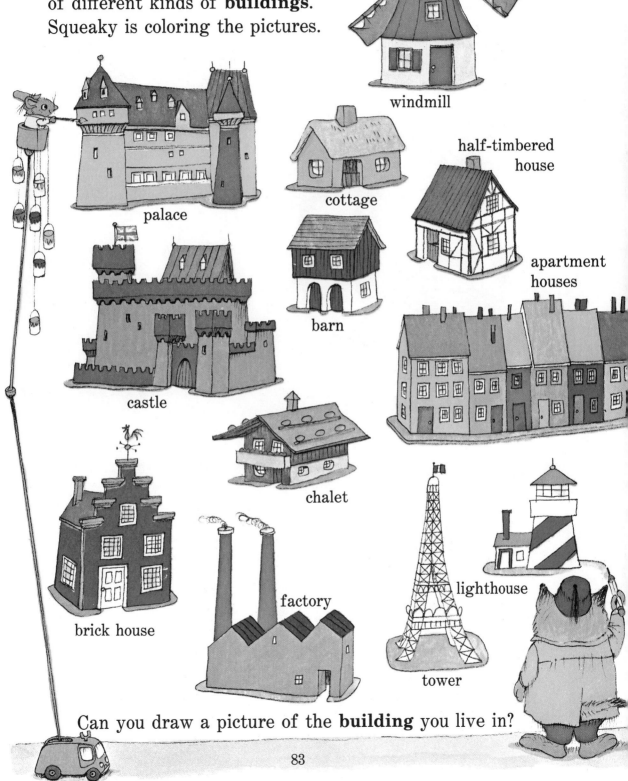

Ali Cat is drawing pictures
of different kinds of **buildings**.
Squeaky is coloring the pictures.

windmill

palace

cottage

half-timbered
house

castle

barn

apartment
houses

chalet

brick house

factory

tower

lighthouse

Can you draw a picture of the **building** you live in?

# A Tale of Tails

WILLY PIG
DID NOT LIKE HIS TAIL.
HE THOUGHT HE WOULD
BE HAPPY IF ONLY HE
HAD A TAIL LIKE A FOX.

No! A FOX TAIL
IS TOO BUSHY FOR A PIG.

IF ONLY HE HAD
A TAIL LIKE A COW.

No! A COW'S TAIL
IS TOO LONG FOR A PIG.

MAYBE IF HE HAD
A BEAUTIFUL GREEN
ALLIGATOR TAIL?

NO! NO! NO!
AN ALLIGATOR'S TAIL
LOOKS SILLY ON A PIG!
WILLY PIG DECIDED THAT
A PIG'S CURLY TAIL
IS THE BEST TAIL,
FOR A PIG.

DON'T YOU THINK SO?

# WHAT
# ANIMALS
# DO

The rooster struts.

The duck waddles.

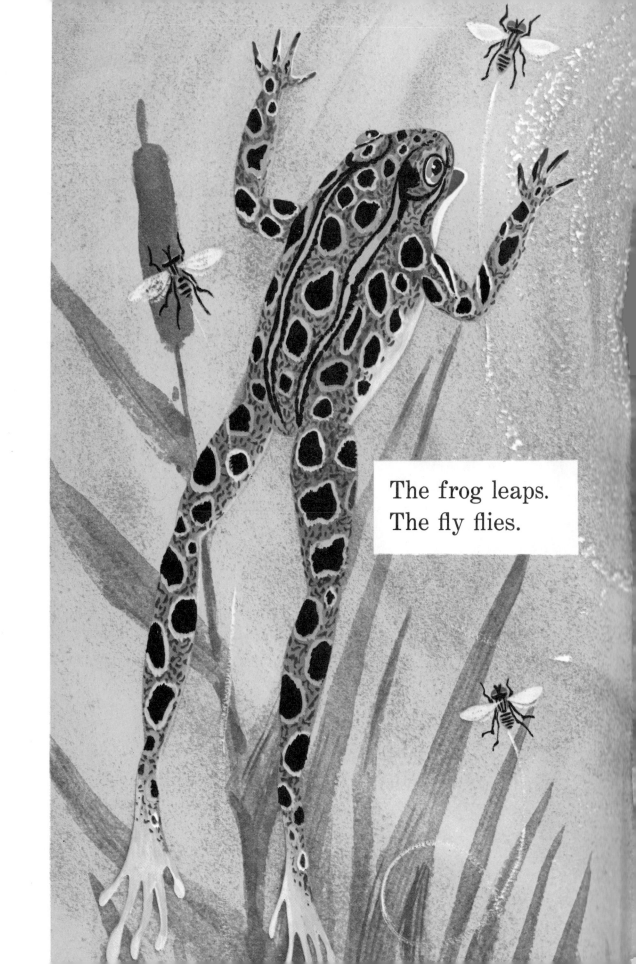

The frog leaps.
The fly flies.

The baby kangaroo rides.

The goose waggles.

The ant
crawls.

The bear shuffles.

The mother kangaroo hops.

And little chicks come
peep-peeping out of their shells.

# More Mother Goose Rhymes

Two little dicky birds,
Sitting on a wall;
One named Peter,
The other named Paul.
Fly away, Peter!
Fly away, Paul!
Come back, Peter!
Come back, Paul!

Little Miss Muffet
Sat on a tuffet,
Eating her curds and whey;
There came a big spider,
Who sat down beside her
And frightened Miss Muffet away.

London Bridge is falling down,
Falling down, falling down,
London Bridge is falling down,
My fair lady.

# MR. HEDGEHOG'S
# CHRISTMAS PRESENT

*by Kathryn Jackson*

London town was even more wonderful than
Mr. Hedgehog had imagined. The stores were
a miracle of shining lights and finery.

Even the mice went about with presents for
their friends, and "Merry Christmas" on their
lips. "I should like to get a present for Mrs.
Hedgehog!" said Mr. Hedgehog to himself.

What should it be?

Not a fur coat. Mrs. Hedgehog had one that
suited her perfectly.

Not a diamond tiara. That would be too heavy for her head. Might make it ache!

Surely not a bottle of scent. Hedgehogs like the smell of fern and hawthorn.

Suddenly something lovely caught Mr. Hedgehog's eye. A bright red apple lay in the clean snow near the curb, lost and forgotten.

Mr. Hedgehog picked it up and brushed off the snow. He polished it with his mittens. Solemnly he offered it to his wife, and said,

"A Merry Christmas, my dear!"

Mrs. Hedgehog kissed him. "Thank you," she said. "I'll make us a big, sweet, warm apple dumpling!"

The little Hedgehogs, one and all, smacked their lips and shouted "Merry Christmas!"

And arm in arm the Hedgehog family hurried home to their cozy burrow, which soon smelled excitingly of apple and spice and crisp pastry browning—the very merriest kind of Christmas smell!

# WHISPER IN MY EAR

One day Elephant went
to visit Mrs. Mouse.
"I am too big to visit
inside your house,"
he said. "Please tell me
what you have inside it."

"First you must be
very quiet," she said.
"Then if you will lift me
up with your trunk, I will
whisper in your ear."

# 1 one

"I have **one** handsome husband inside my house," said Mrs. Mouse. "He is helping me do the housework."

one

One handsome husband.
Is he helping with the housework?

# 2 two

"In my kitchen I have **two** pots. In one pot I cook meat and in the other pot I cook vegetables." "It smells delicious," said Elephant.

one    two

Here are her two pots cooking meat and vegetables.
Mr. Mouse is tasting to see if the vegetables are done.

# 3 three

"How many beds do you have
in your house?" asked Elephant.
"I have **three** beds,"
said Mrs. Mouse in a whisper.

one

two

three

Mr. Mouse likes to make his own bed.

# 4 four

"I have **four** clocks
that tell the time.
My favorite one
is the cuckoo clock."

Sometimes it
frightens Mr. Mouse.

one

two

three

four

# 5 five

"In the evening when it gets dark, **five** lamps make my little house light and cheery," she said.

one

two

three

four

five

Mr. Mouse is very good at dusting the five lamps.

# 6 six

"In my house I have **six** chairs," whispered Mrs. Mouse. "Some are hard and some are soft."

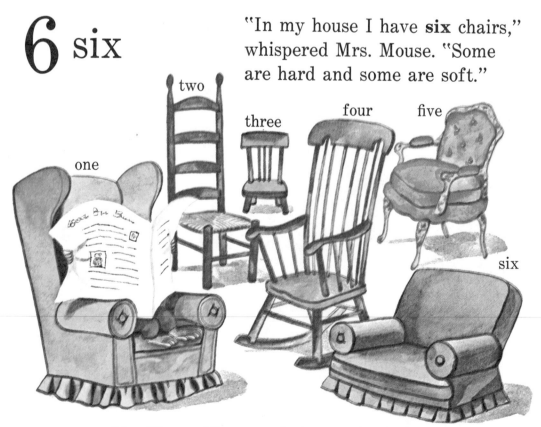

one

two

three

four

five

six

Mr. Mouse likes to sit in a soft chair.

# 7 seven

"I have **seven** pretty hats,"
she whispered in Elephant's ear.

Mr. Mouse is trying on one of her hats.

# 8 eight

"I am a very neat housewife.
I have **eight** brooms to help me
keep the house clean," she whispered.

Mr. Mouse is sweeping the floor.

# 9 nine

"To make my house look pretty, I have **nine** plants which I water every day."

one

two

three

four

five

six

seven

eight

nine

Oh, dear! Mrs. Mouse forgot to water one of her nine plants today.

# 10 ten

"I have **ten** books which I like to read,"
she whispered to Elephant.
"What are the names of your books?" asked Elephant.

one

two

three

four

five

six

seven

eight

nine

ten

Mr. Mouse likes to read books, too.
What is he reading about?

107

# 11 eleven

"I have **eleven** beautiful pictures hanging on my wall," she whispered.

ten

three

seven

one

nine

six

eleven

two

eight

five

four

"You certainly have a very nice house," said Elephant. "But why do you have to whisper in my ear?"

"Oh, I have to whisper," said Mrs. Mouse in a whisper, "because I have **twelve** darling children who are fast asleep in the bedroom."

# 12 twelve

Can you count **twelve** children taking their naps?
Why don't you whisper in Mrs. Mouse's ear and
tell her that the children have finished
their naps and want to go out to play?

THANK YOU!

# A CASTLE IN DENMARK

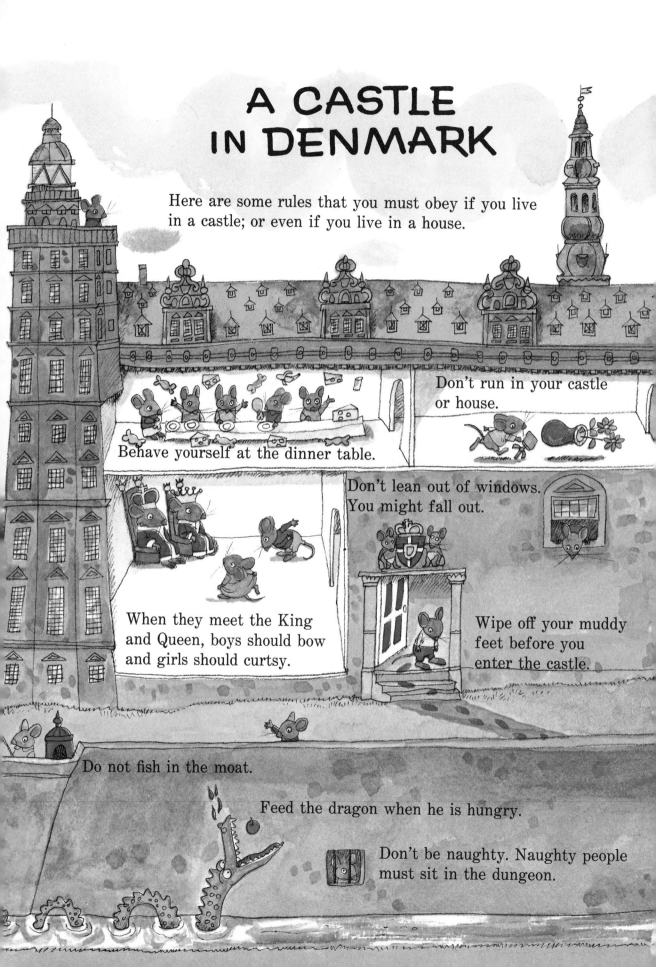

Here are some rules that you must obey if you live in a castle; or even if you live in a house.

Behave yourself at the dinner table.

Don't run in your castle or house.

Don't lean out of windows. You might fall out.

When they meet the King and Queen, boys should bow and girls should curtsy.

Wipe off your muddy feet before you enter the castle.

Do not fish in the moat.

Feed the dragon when he is hungry.

Don't be naughty. Naughty people must sit in the dungeon.

Keep a light burning, so that the witches who live in your castle can find their way home at night.

Be careful where you fly your kite.

Don't land your helicopter on the roof.

All ghosts must put their sheets in the washing machine when they get dirty.

All witches must put their brooms away when they have finished with them.

Keep your suit of armor well oiled so that you won't squeak.

Don't leave things on the stairs where people can trip on them.

Don't shoot the cannons without permission.

Don't climb inside cannons unless you are a cannonball.

Don't let down the drawbridge to strangers.

If you are coming to visit make sure the drawbridge is down before you try to cross it.

# CARS AND TRUCKS

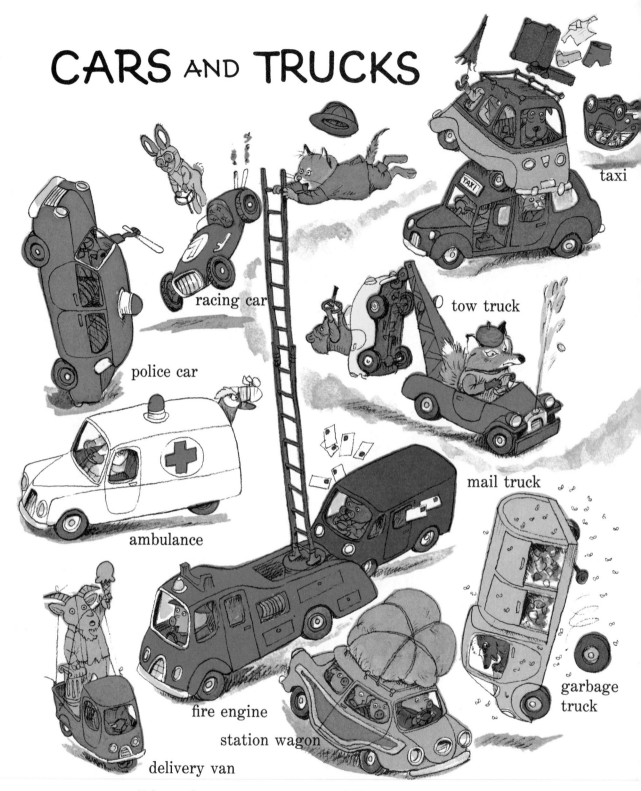

taxi

racing car

tow truck

police car

mail truck

ambulance

fire engine

station wagon

garbage truck

delivery van

Dingo has a new automobile,
a shiny red racing car.
Look out, all you other automobiles.
Look out, trucks and busses and fire engines.

jeep

windshield
headlight
taillight
bumper
wheel
steering wheel
tire

trailer truck

bus

motorcycle

motor scooter

policeman

traffic light

dump truck

sports car

sedan

direction sign

double decker bus

Oh that Dingo! He is very naughty
to be such a nuisance, isn't he?
Ali Cat is quietly painting a poster.
Can you read the words on the poster?

# More Cars and Trucks

A taxi will take us anywhere we want to go in a hurry.

The oldtime "tin lizzie" was loved by many people. It was the most popular car of its day.

The police car patrols the streets to help keep us all safe.

The fire chief's car whizzes by on the way to a fire.

The station wagon used to look like this. Part of it was made of sturdy, polished wood.

A sports car is smaller than most cars and can go very fast.

The tow truck tows the wrecked car to the garage to be fixed.

WE FIX IT

The sturdy jeep can go places other cars can't go, up hill or down hill or in mud or sand.

The back part of the dump truck tips up and dumps its load.

The gasoline truck brings gasoline to the filling station.

A racing car is very high powered and goes very fast. Its engine makes a loud roar.

The happy little nursery-school bus takes children to and from their nursery school.

Sooner or later most cars end up like this.

# THE FOX AND
# THE CROW

*Told by Patricia Scarry*

A crow sat in a high tree holding a tasty bit of cheese in her mouth.

Along came a hungry wart hog.

"The crow will laugh when she sees my funny face," he said. "And when she laughs, she'll drop the cheese."

He called to the crow, making a funny face.

But she didn't even smile.

Along came a hungry little elephant.

"Drop the cheese to me, Crow," said the elephant, "or I will give you a shower bath!"

But the crow did not drop the cheese, even though WHOOSH! the elephant's trunk sent up a stream of water.

"Drop the cheese to me," called the big brown bear, "and you may have this pot of honey."

But the crow did not like honey, and she did not drop the cheese.

The crow was about to eat the cheese when along came a cunning little fox.

"Oh beautiful crow," he called, "you are lovely to see. A bird with such charming feathers must sing a pretty tune. Please sing for me."

Now the crow had never been told she was pretty, although she thought she was. And she had never been told that her voice was pretty.

She opened her beak and rasped an ugly CAAW!

Down tumbled the cheese, into the fox's mouth!

Now wasn't she a silly bird to let that sweet talk fool her?

# More
# Mother Goose
# Rhymes

There was an old woman tossed up in a basket,
Seventeen times as high as the moon;
Where she was going I couldn't but ask it,
For under her arm she carried a broom.
Old woman, old woman, old woman, said I,
Where are you going to up so high?
To sweep the cobwebs out of the sky,
And I'll be with you by-and-by.

# WHEN YOU GROW UP

What would you like to be
when you are a bigger?
Would you like to be
a good cook like your father?
Or would you like to be
a doctor or a nurse?
What would you like to be?

police officer      fire fighter

nurse      milkman      farmer

carpenter      musician

cowboy

dentist      secretary      good cook

singer

artist

pilot

truck driver

teacher

train conductor

commuter

store keeper

dancer

daddy

mommy

# COUSCOUS,
## ᵀᴴᴱ ALGERIAN DETECTIVE

Couscous was the best detective in Algiers. He was very good at disguising himself to look like someone else.

Couscous was in disguise as he walked past the robber's den of Pepe le Gangstair. He was trying to think of a way to get inside the robber's den and capture Pepe and his band of dirty rats.

Can you tell which one is Couscous? No! You can't—because Couscous is so good at disguising himself!

Suddenly Couscous had a good idea. He hurried back to the police station, where his cat and mouse assistants were waiting. He took off his disguise and told them of his plan.

"You have a very clever plan, Couscous!" they all agreed.

That night when it was dark, a small group came
to the door of the robber's den and knocked.
Knock! Knock! Knock!

"Who is knocking at my door?" growled Pepe le Gangstair.

"It is I, the pretty dancing girl Fatima, with my troupe of musicians," a soft sweet voice answered. "We have come to entertain you."

"Come in, come in," said Pepe. He opened the door and let them in.

Oh, how beautifully Fatima danced! She was magnificent!

"MORE! MORE!" shouted Pepe.

"I have more for you," said Fatima, "but first I must blindfold you, as I have a big surprise."

So she blindfolded Pepe and the robbers and led them out of the door. . . .

. . . into the police wagon!

The robbers were prisoners! They had been captured by that clever master of disguise COUSCOUS!!!

My! That Couscous is a clever fellow.

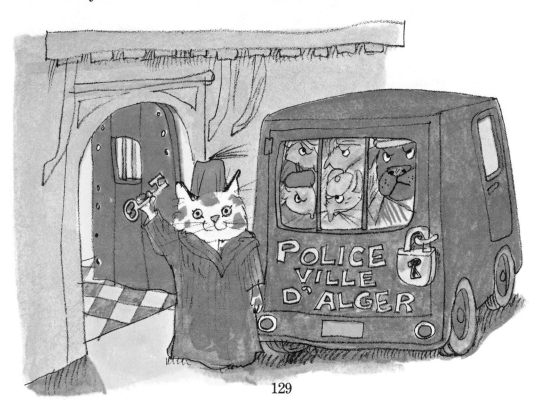

# Tom, the Fishing Cat

TOM CAT WENT FISHING.

HE CAUGHT A LITTLE FISH!

HE CAUGHT A BIGGER FISH!

LOOK! THERE IS
A GREAT BIG ONE!

LOOK OUT, TOM!

NOW
WHO WAS CAUGHT?

# Count with Hooty Owl

HOOTY OWL AND HIS MOTHER WENT TO THE STORE AND BOUGHT ONE PIECE OF CHEESE

THEY BOUGHT TWO ORANGES

AND THREE APPLES.

MOTHER OWL PICKED OUT FOUR WHITE EGGS.

WHAT COULD BE NICER FOR SUPPER THAN FIVE ONIONS?

SIX PICKLES, MAYBE?

THEY BOUGHT SEVEN FAT HOT DOGS FROM THE BUTCHER.

AND THEN, HOME THEY WENT FOR SUPPER.

SEVEN
SIX
FIVE
FOUR
THREE
TWO
ONE....? "WHAT BECAME OF ?" THAT ONE PIECE OF CHEESE. ASKED MOTHER, WITH A SMILE. I THINK SHE KNEW. DON'T YOU?

# More Mother Goose Rhymes

Elsie Marley is grown so fine,
She won't get up to feed the swine,
But lies in bed till eight or nine,
Lazy Elsie Marley.

133

# THE HUNGRY
# BEGGARS

The beggars smelled something cooking in
Mamma Bear's kitchen. Mamma Bear had baked a cake.

Mamma Bear told them she would give them each a piece
if they would mind the house while she went shopping.
My! That is hard cake, Mamma!

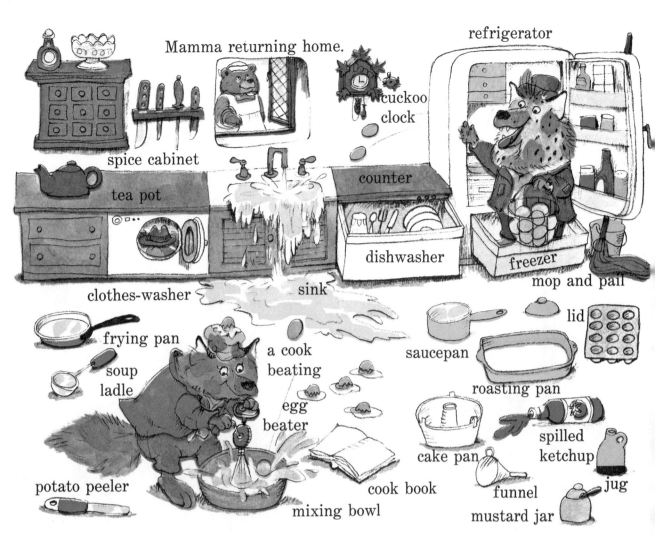

Mamma returning home.

refrigerator

cuckoo clock

spice cabinet

tea pot

counter

dishwasher

freezer

mop and pail

clothes-washer

sink

frying pan

soup ladle

a cook beating

egg beater

saucepan

lid

roasting pan

cake pan

spilled ketchup

jug

potato peeler

cook book

mixing bowl

funnel

mustard jar

The beggars decided to make a soft cake
while Mamma was out. They were going to
surprise her with it when she returned.

Mamma surprised the beggars. She made them
go to work and clean up the mess they had made.

# IN THE FLOWER GARDEN

worm

bird

birdhouse

The bunnies love to grow flowers. They spray the flowers to keep the bugs from eating them. They water them to make them grow. Which flower do you like the best?

black-eyed Susan

rose

thistle

daisy

seedling

bee

lady's-slipper

clover

tulip

buttercup

seed

daffodil

narcissus

dandelion

violet

morning-glory

zinnia

hollyhock

foxglove

bluet

pink

aster

insect-spray can

bluebell

sweet William

petunia

pansy

beetle

flower basket

watering can

trowel

cultivator

lily of the valley

flower pot

137

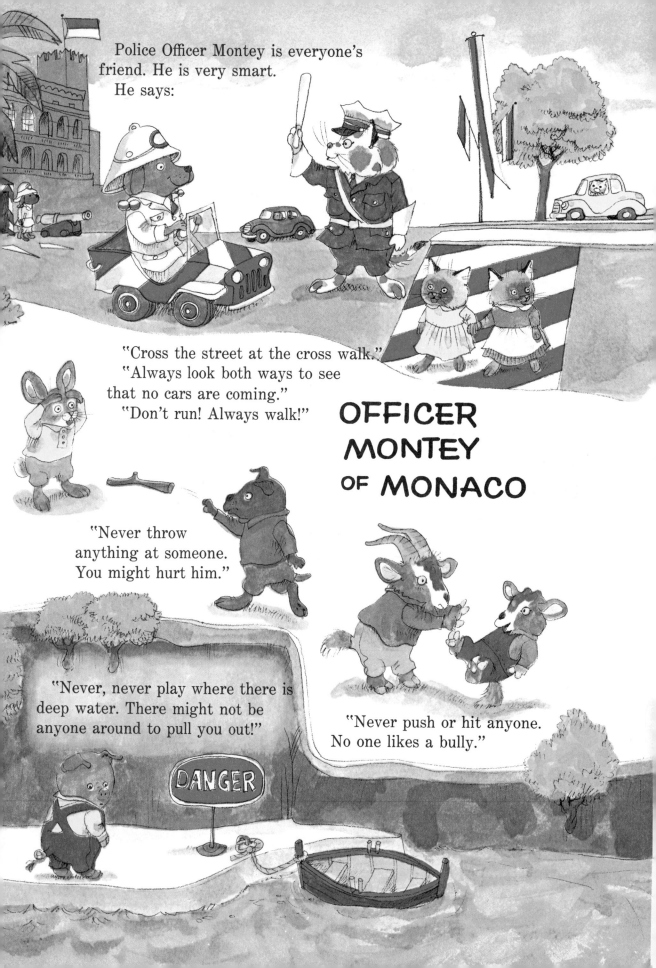

Police Officer Montey is everyone's friend. He is very smart. He says:

"Cross the street at the cross walk."
"Always look both ways to see that no cars are coming."
"Don't run! Always walk!"

# OFFICER MONTEY OF MONACO

"Never throw anything at someone. You might hurt him."

"Never, never play where there is deep water. There might not be anyone around to pull you out!"

"Never push or hit anyone. No one likes a bully."

DANGER

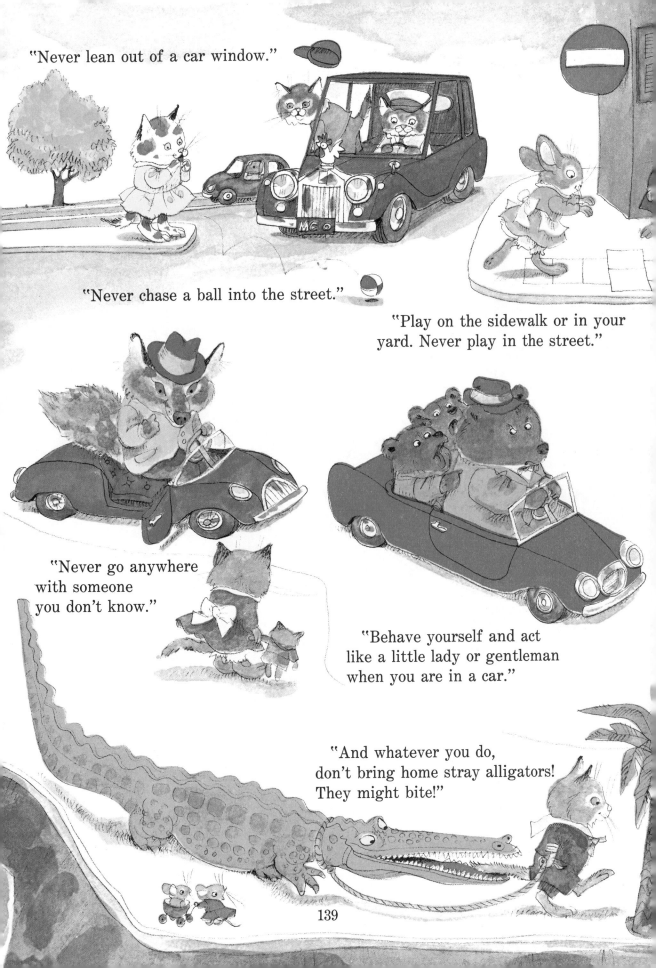

"Never lean out of a car window."

"Never chase a ball into the street."

"Play on the sidewalk or in your yard. Never play in the street."

"Never go anywhere with someone you don't know."

"Behave yourself and act like a little lady or gentleman when you are in a car."

"And whatever you do, don't bring home stray alligators! They might bite!"

# IS THIS THE HOUSE
# OF MISTRESS MOUSE?

This is the house
of Mister Mouse.
He lived all alone
and he was very lonely.
One day he received a
letter from Mistress Mouse.
The letter said:
"Dear Mister Mouse,
I am very lonely too.
Will you please come
and visit me?
Love and kisses,
Mistress Mouse."

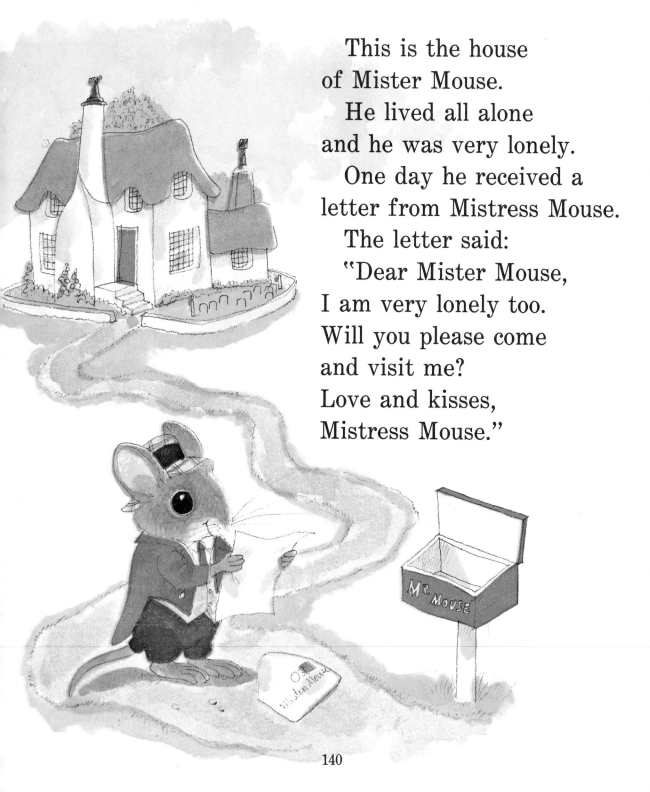

Mister Mouse said to himself,
"I would like very much to visit Mistress Mouse but I don't know where she lives.
"However, I will just have to get into my little car and go look for her."

"There is a house just ahead,"
said Mister Mouse. "Perhaps that is
where Mistress Mouse lives."

He knocked on the door.

"Is this the house of Mistress Mouse?" he asked.

Mister Mouse was very frightened for that was the house of . . .

"*MEOWWWRRR!*"

. . . the house of
Mister CAT!

"What a cute little
mouse," thought
Mister Cat as he
watched him speed
away in his car.
"I wonder why he
was so frightened?"
But Mister Mouse
knew better than
to go into Mister
Cat's house. Didn't he?

Soon he came to a bright red barn.
He knocked on the barn door. It was
the house of . . .

"CUT-CUT-CUT-CU-DAHCUT"

. . . it was the house of Mrs. HEN and her baby chicks.

"Please don't bother me. I am teaching my chicks to scratch," she said.

HOW TO SCRATCH

And so Mister Mouse traveled on until he came to a big castle house. He knocked on the castle door.

It was the castle of . . .

# "ROARRRRR !!!"

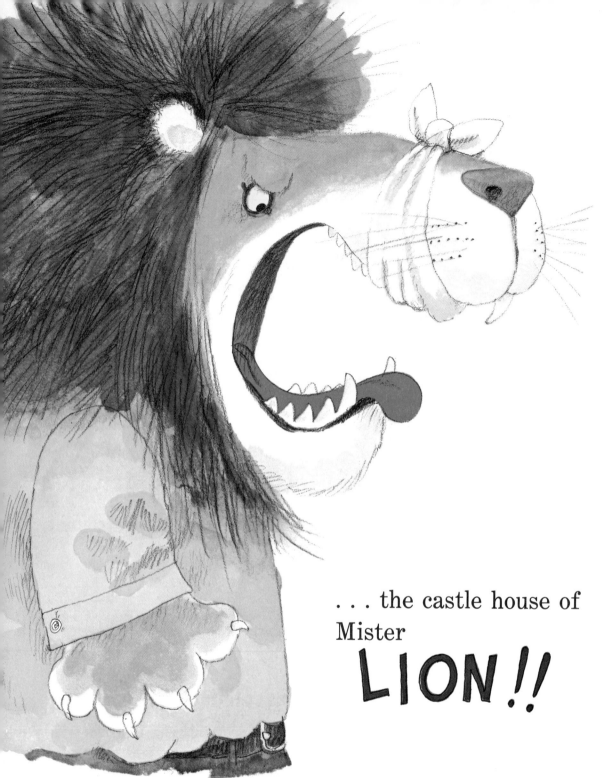

. . . the castle house of Mister **LION!!**

He was in a very bad temper because he had a very bad toothache. Mister Mouse raced away as fast as he could go!

Finally he came to a cute little house on a lovely country lane.

He knocked on the pretty little yellow door.

"Is this the house of Mistress Mouse?" he asked.

The door slowly opened.

Sure enough! It WAS the house of
Mistress Mouse!

Mistress Mouse was so happy to see him.
And Mister Mouse was so happy to see her.

"Will you marry me so that we will never
again be lonely?" asked Mister Mouse.

"Why, YES! " said Mistress Mouse.

And so they were married by Preacher Mole.
Mister Mouse gave Mistress Mouse a golden
wedding ring with a bright diamond on top.

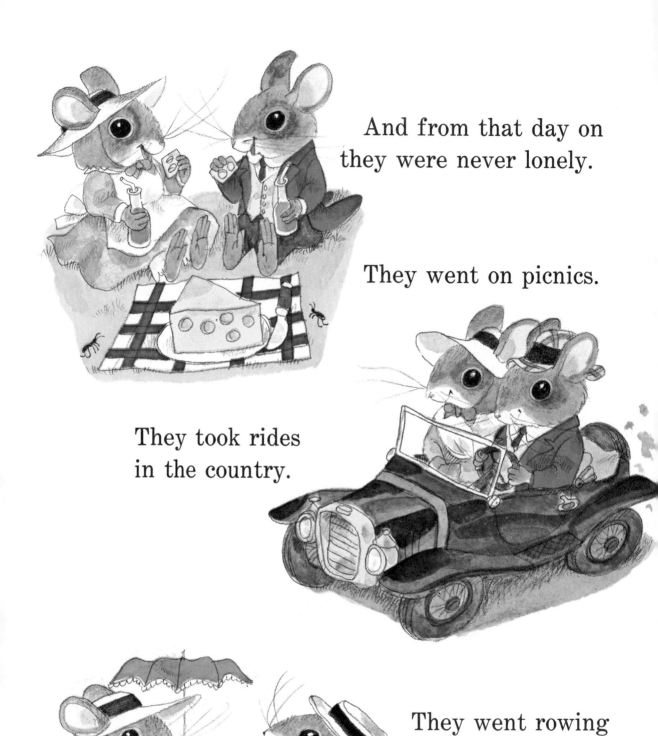

And from that day on they were never lonely.

They went on picnics.

They took rides in the country.

They went rowing on the lake.

And then one night, after they had finished
their supper, they heard something.

It was a tiny "Squeak, squeak, squeak,"
coming from the bedroom.

What do you suppose it was that was
squeaking?

It was their **BABY!**
He wanted to be kissed good night.
"Good night, Daddy Mouse."
"Good night, Mommy Mouse."
"Good night, Baby Mouse."
"Good night."

# COLORS

This color is yellow.

Baby chicks are yellow.
Daffodils are yellow, too.

This color is blue.

Bunny's sailor
suit is blue.

The sky is blue.

This color is red.

An apple is red.

This tricycle is red.

Blue and yellow make green.

A fat frog is green.

In summer,
leaves are green.

# Red and yellow make orange.

Bunny's carrot
is orange.

A pumpkin is orange, too.

Blue and red make purple.

Violets and pansies are purple.

Grapes and plums are purple.

This color is brown.

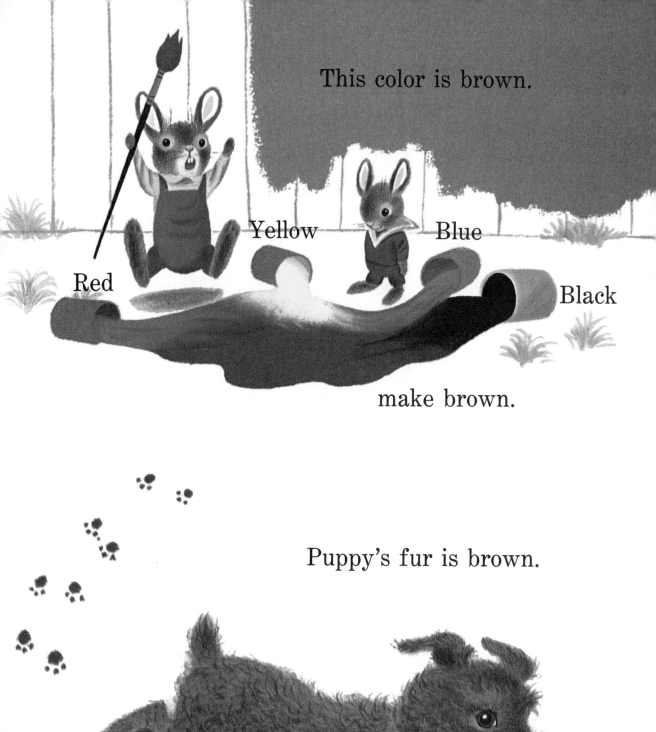

Red    Yellow    Blue    Black

make brown.

Puppy's fur is brown.

This little pony
is brown, too.

Red and white
make pink.

Roses and
bunny noses are pink.

Baby pigs are pink.

This is white.

A snowman is white, and so is a duck.

This is black.

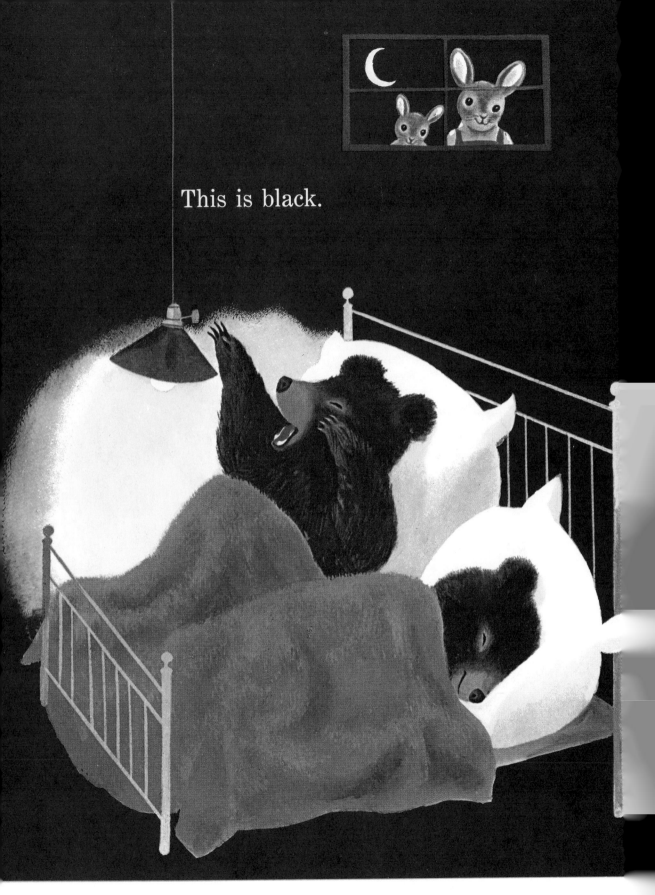

Sleepy bear cubs are black.

Red, yellow, blue, green—
a parrot has many colors.

Which is your favorite color?

# CLOTHES

Wiggles' clothes are
scattered all about.
Wiggles is looking
for his other mitten.
It's right where you
put it, Wiggles.

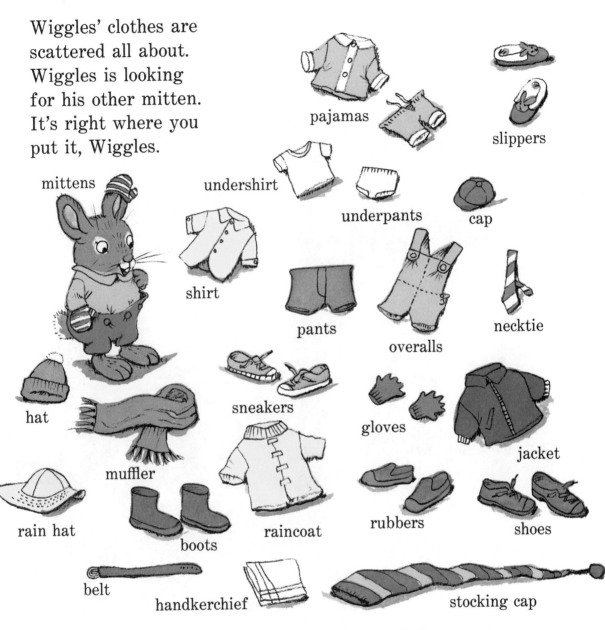

pajamas

slippers

mittens

undershirt

underpants

cap

shirt

pants

overalls

necktie

sneakers

gloves

jacket

hat

muffler

rubbers

shoes

rain hat

boots

raincoat

belt

handkerchief

stocking cap

Why can't you hang up your clothes
neatly the way your sister does?

stockings  blouse

skirt

slip

panties

pinafore

nightgown

173

# More Mother Goose Rhymes

Charley, Charley,
Stole the barley
Out of the baker's shop.
The baker came out
And gave him a clout,
Which made poor Charley hop.

Little Boy Blue,
Come blow your horn,
The sheep's in the meadow,
The cow's in the corn;
But where is the little boy
Tending the sheep?
He's under a haycock,
Fast asleep.
Will you wake him?
No, not I,
For if I do,
He's sure to cry.

One misty, moisty morning,
When cloudy was the weather,
There I met an old man
Clothed all in leather;
Clothed all in leather,
With cap under his chin.
How do you do, and how do you do,
And how do you do again?

# AT THE AIRPORT

weather instruments

blimp

microphone

control tower

helicopter

baggage train

waiting room

binoculars

tourist camera

observation deck

The man in the control tower is talking
into his microphone. He is talking to the
handsome pilot by radio. He is telling him
that he will have nice weather on his flight.

jet plane

wind sock

runway

hangar

runway lights

light plane

propeller

mechanic

jet military plane

handsome
pilot

jet passenger plane

tail

baggage man

pretty
stewardess

fuselage

wing

baggage
loader

jet engine

passenger-loading
stairs

# Airplanes

## THE FIRST AIRPLANES

The very first heavier-than-air machine that would really fly was built by the Wright Brothers at Kitty Hawk, North Carolina.

Henri Farman, in France, flew his little biplane a distance of one mile. It was one of the first city-to-city flights.

The first important flight over water was made by Louis Blériot, a Frenchman. He flew across the English Channel.

The first light plane built in Europe was the tiny *"Demoiselle."*

A few years after the Wright Brothers' famous flight, Glenn Curtiss built successful airplanes.

The flimsy little *"Vin Fizz Flyer"* made the first flight across the United States.

# WORLD WAR I FIGHTER PLANES

The black crosses painted
on this Fokker monoplane show
that it was German.

The Fokker triplane had
three sets of wings.

The Spad was
flown by American pilots.

The Albatros was the prize of
German fighter squadrons.

The Voisin was a French
observation plane.

The Sopwith Camel was
the fastest of the British fighters.

# WORLD WAR II
# FIGHTER PLANES

Messerschmitt 109,
Germany

P-51 Mustang,
U.S.A.

Spitfire,
Great Britain

# JET PLANES

The jet jeep is a small, U.S. Army
helicopter. It is very useful.

Jet fighter planes can travel
faster than the speed of sound.

Jet passenger planes are
very fast and comfortable.

# Harry's Airplane Ride

HARRY CLIMBED
INTO HIS AIRPLANE.

UP, UP, UP,
INTO THE SKY HE FLEW.

BUT
SOMETHING WAS WRONG!

GOOD GRACIOUS!
HE WAS FALLING
STRAIGHT DOWN!

MRS. PIG WAS HANGING
HER LAUNDRY OUT TO DRY.

HARRY WAS SAVED
BY MRS. PIG'S PANTIES!
HE IS LUCKY, ISN'T HE?

# PIERRE,
## THE PARIS POLICEMAN

Pierre was directing traffic when
suddenly he heard someone shout,
"Stop that robber! Stop that robber!"
A robber had stolen some jewels from
a store. The robber ran to his car.

Pierre hopped on his bicycle and chased after the robber. He blew his whistle furiously. Brrrrrrreeeeeeeeeet!

Through the crowded streets they raced.

AVENUE DES VOLEURS

Restaurant ☆☆☆
QUATRE ÉTOILE

Suddenly
the robber's
car crashed into a
sidewalk cafe. The robber
ran into the restaurant.
    Brrrrrrrrrreeeeeeeeeeet!

Pierre followed him.
Brrrrrrrrrreeeeeeeeeet. . . .

. . . into the kitchen.
"Where is the robber?"
he roared at the chef.
The chef hadn't seen any robber.

Poor Pierre! He had lost
the robber.
"Mmmmmmm, that soup
you are cooking smells good,"
said Pierre. "May I taste it?"

187

He put in his paw.
Look at what he found!
The robber! The robber
had hidden in the soup.

Before Pierre took
the robber away
to be punished, they
all had some soup.

"This is the best
soup ever!" said the chef
to the robber.
"Perhaps after you
have been punished for
stealing, you will come back
and help me make soup
all the time? We will call
it 'Robber Soup.'"

Everyone thought that
that was a good idea.

# More Mother Goose Rhymes

Three little kittens,
They lost their mittens,
And they began to cry,
Oh, mother dear, we sadly fear
Our mittens we have lost.
What! lost your mittens,
You naughty kittens!
Then you shall have no pie.

The three little kittens,
They found their mittens,
And they began to cry,
Oh, mother dear, see here, see here,
Our mittens we have found.
Put on your mittens, You silly kittens,
And you shall have some pie.

The three little kittens
Put on their mittens,
And soon ate up the pie;
Oh, mother dear, we greatly fear
Our mittens we have soiled.
What! soiled your mittens,
You naughty kittens!
Then they began to sigh.

The three little kittens,
They washed their mittens,
And hung them out to dry;
Oh! mother dear, do you not hear
Our mittens we have washed?
What! washed your mittens,
Then you're good kittens.
But I smell a rat close by.

# A NICE SURPRISE

If I write a letter

and mail it

to someone I love,

someone I love may write a letter to me.

190

# POLITE ELEPHANT

Everyone likes the polite elephant.
He knows the right things to say and do.
   When the polite elephant waits for the bus,
he takes his place in line. He never pushes
or shoves.

Sometimes
the bus
is crowded.

Sometimes the polite elephant goes visiting.
When someone comes
to the door, he tips
his hat and says,
"Hello, Mrs. Smith.

How are you?"

192

The polite elephant always
offers his seat to a lady.

The polite elephant is a
good guest. He knows that
some rooms are for sitting
. . . and others are
for playing.

When it's time for
the polite elephant
to go home,
he remembers
to thank his friends.
"Thank you,"
he says. "I've had
a nice time."

The polite elephant
is polite at home,
too. He always washes
his hands and face
before sitting at
the table.

He sits straight in his chair. When
he wants something, he says, "Please."
When he gets it, he says, "Thank you."

Sometimes the polite
elephant's friends come
to his house. He greets
them at the door.
"Hello," he says.
"Please come in."

He introduces them
to his mother. "Mommy,
this is Jimmy."

The polite elephant is a good playmate.
He shares his toys with
his friends. And he is
very careful when he plays
with someone else's toys.

When his friends leave, the polite elephant goes to the door with them.

"Thank you for coming," he says.

If you should ever meet the polite elephant, he'll be just as polite to you. He'll tip his hat and say, "How do you do?"

CROSS WALK

# CHIPMUNK'S
# BIRTHDAY
# PARTY

It was Chipmunk's birthday.

He invited his friends to come to his
birthday party.

When they came he said,

"Hi, Rabbit! Hi, Mouse!
Hi, Goat! Hi, Donkey!
Hi, Frogs!"

199

"Now just a minute." said Mommy
Chipmunk. "There'll be no birthday party
until your ears are clean!"

Bunny Rabbit has big ears to clean,
hasn't he?

Chipmunk and Mouse helped Mommy in the kitchen. Mommies always have to work hard when they give birthday parties.

MOUSE! What are you doing? Can't you wait until the party begins?

All the children went outside to play.

Chipmunk went sailing on the pond with Rabbit. They wore life jackets. They wanted to be safe just in case they should fall overboard.

Chipmunk chased butterflies with his net.
He was not a very good butterfly chaser.

Then they all played leapfrog.

Hide-and-seek was the next game.
Chipmunk was "it."
He tried to find his friends.
Can you find Mouse?
Where is he hiding?

It was time to stop playing games.

It was time to eat ice cream and drink lemonade. They put on funny hats. Froggie played his oboe.

Mouse picked some flowers.

He gave them to Mommy Chipmunk to thank her for the birthday party. What a nice Mouse! Do you have nice birthday parties, too?

# THE BUNNY BOOK

*by Patricia Scarry*

The Daddy Bunny tossed his baby in the air.

"What will our baby be when he grows up?" asked the Daddy Bunny.

Baby Bunny sat in his basket and smiled at his bunny family. He knew what he would be.

"Maybe he will be a nice little mailman who will bring a letter to every house and make the neighbors happy," said Daddy Bunny.

A hungry little bunny cousin wished that the baby would have a candy store.

"He could make lollypops with funny faces and give them to all the good children," wished the hungry little bunny cousin.

211

Great Uncle Bunny wanted the baby to be an engineer on a big train.

"He would ring the bell when he was ready to start the train. And blow his horn, Toot! Toot! in the tunnels," said Great Uncle Bunny.

But the baby bunny did not want to be a
mailman or a candy man or an engineer on a
big train when he grew up. He nibbled on his
carrot and looked wise. He knew what he
wanted to be.

"I think our baby
bunny should be an
airplane pilot," said the
little bunny sister.
"What fun to jump
out of his plane
in a parachute!"

"Maybe he will be a
fireman," said Great Aunt
Bunny. "He could drive a
big truck to all the fires."

"He may grow
up to be a
farmer with
a fine red
tractor," said
Uncle Bunny.

214

But the baby bunny did not want to be a fireman or an airplane pilot or a farmer with a fine red tractor when he grew up.

He bounced on his daddy's knee and laughed. Can you guess what he will be?

He will have lots of little bunny children to feed when they are hungry. He will read them a story when they are sleepy, and tuck them into bed at night.

And that is what the baby bunny will grow up to be. A daddy rabbit.

# More Mother Goose Rhymes

There was a crow sat on a stone,
When he was gone,
Then there was none.

Here am I,
Little jumping Joan;
When nobody's with me
I'm all alone.

There was an old crow
Sat upon a clod:
That's the end of my song,
That's odd.

Baa, baa, black sheep,
Have you any wool?
Yes, sir, yes, sir,
Three bags full;
One for my master,
And one for my dame,
And one for the little boy
Who lives down the lane.

Diddle, diddle, dumpling, my son John,
Went to bed with his trousers on;
One shoe off, and one shoe on;
Diddle, diddle, dumpling, my son John.

Jack, be nimble,
Jack, be quick,
Jack, jump over
The candlestick.

To market, to market, to buy a fat pig,
Home again, home again, jiggety-jig;
To market, to market, to buy a fat hog,
Home again, home again, jiggety-jog.

As I went to Bonner,
I met a pig
Without a wig,
Upon my word and honor.

Hey diddle, diddle,
The cat and the fiddle,
The cow jumped over the moon;
The little dog laughed
To see such sport,
And the dish ran away with the spoon.

# Boats

Christopher Columbus sailed
to America in the year 1492
on the "*Santa Maria.*"

The Pilgrims sailed to America
on the "*Mayflower.*"

Pirates used to sail the seas
in search of treasure ships.

Many sailors like to row a little rowboat.

An outboard motorboat speeds over the waves.

A sport fishing boat is used for deep-sea fishing.

The racing boat skims the top of the water.

Wind blowing on the sails makes a sailboat go.

People may eat and sleep on their motor cruisers on a long trip.

ferry boat

ocean liner

barge

speedboat

submarine

oar

leaky rowboat

# MORE BOATS

Mr. Fixit's **boat** has a hole in the bottom. Water is coming in through the hole and filling the **boat**. It will sink. Mr. Fixit is drilling another hole because he thinks the water will empty out through it. Isn't he silly?

a singing gondolier

gondola

# Tugboat Tom

TUGBOAT TOM WAS
BRINGING A BIG SHIP
INTO THE HARBOR.

SUDDENLY
HE HEARD A CRY
FOR HELP!

WAS IT A SAILBOAT SINKING?
NO!

WAS IT A FREIGHTER
CUT IN TWO?
NO! GUESS WHAT!.....

IT WAS BIG HILDA!
SHE HAD GONE OUT
TOO FAR ON HER
TOY HORSE!

SHE IS BIG ENOUGH
TO KNOW BETTER
THAN TO DO THAT.
ISN'T SHE?

# GOOD LUCK IN ROME

Federico and Maria were visiting Rome for the very first time.
They had heard of a fountain which is supposed to bring you
good luck if you throw a coin into it.

Federico stopped his car and got out to ask two carabinieri
how to get there.

Now for some reason which can't be explained . . .

. . . Federico's car started off without him! Maria didn't know how to stop it! "Follow that car!" Federico said to a taxi driver.

"Help! Help!" said Maria.

Into St. Peter's Square the little car raced.
The Swiss Guards were called out to stop it.
But they were too late.

229

Down the Spanish Steps
they tumbled.

230

Down narrow streets . . .
. . . into the very fountain
they were looking for.

"You will surely have
good luck," said the
carabinieri. "Most
people have good luck
by putting only a
penny in the fountain.
But look! You have
put your car in! Yes,
you will surely
have good luck!"

# THE FIREMEN TO THE RESCUE

rescue truck

police car

nozzle

rear-wheel steerer

fire engine

hook-and-ladder truck

front-wheel steerer

hose

boots

helmet

first-aid kit

hook

fire-alarm box

A beautiful lady is screaming at her
window. Her house is on fire!
Clang clang! The fire engines,
filled with brave firemen,
are coming to the rescue.

232

ambulance

flames

water

smoke

fire chief

beautiful screaming lady

megaphone

fire chief's car

brave hero

pumper

fire hydrant

jumping gentleman

ladder

firemen

rescue net

fire extinguisher

Look at the hero climbing the ladder.
I think he will be able to save
the beautiful lady, don't you?

233

# THINGS WE DO

There are many things
that we can do. And there
are some things we cannot do.
What is one thing we can't do?
Look and see.

dig

build

break

sleep

walk

run

stand

read

watch

kick

234

pull

push

talk

listen

shout

whisper

laugh

smile

cry

jump over

crawl under

fall down

eat

we can't fly

tip a hat

go up

go down

go in

come out

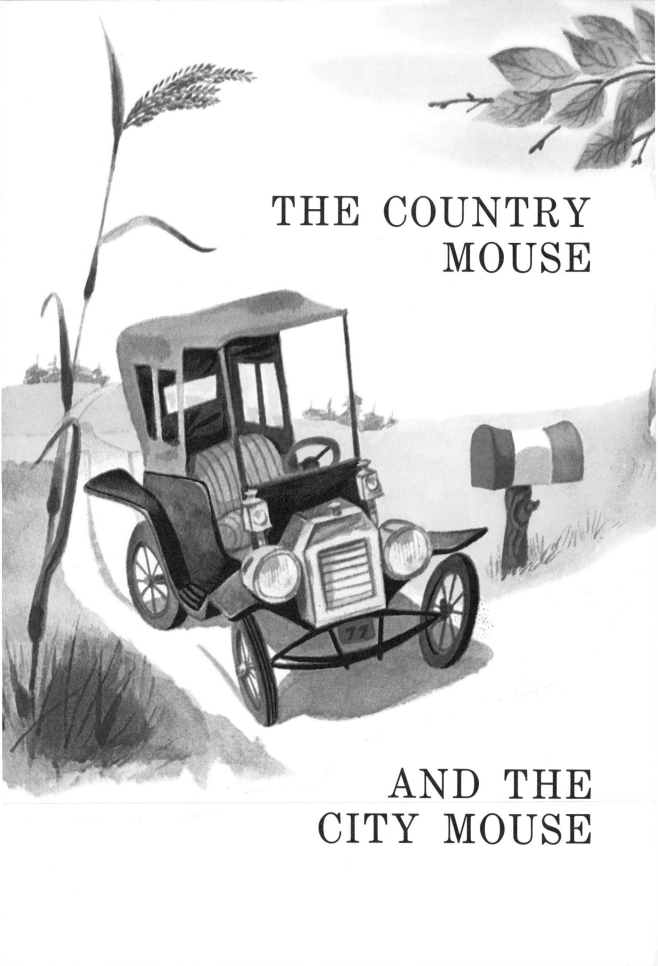

# THE COUNTRY MOUSE

# AND THE CITY MOUSE

*Told by Patricia Scarry*

Annie Mouse lived quietly in the country. One day her friend from the city came to visit her. Annie was delighted.

"Melissa dear, welcome to the country!" she said. "Do come in!"

Annie Mouse asked some friends in for lunch. But Melissa did not eat one nibble of the meal Annie proudly served.

"In the city I dine on spice cake and wine," said the city mouse, rather grandly.

"In the city I have
a machine that plays
music, and I dance
on a velvet carpet,"
said Melissa.

"Oh Annie, won't you leave this dull country
life behind, and come to the city with me?"

"My, it does sound tempting," said Annie.

So Annie rode off to the city with her friend.
Honk! Honk! Beep! Beep! Toot! Toot!
"Please drive slowly," begged Annie.
"Can't hear a word," screamed Melissa.
"Isn't it marvelous fun?"

Melissa's home in the city was beautiful.
And such fun to explore! Gaily they raced down
the hall.

Suddenly, WHOOF! barked a fierce, angry
voice.

"Help! It's the dog!" squeaked Melissa.

And the two friends ran, shaking with
fright.

They slammed the dining-room door, just in time. The poor country mouse almost fainted with fear.

But Melissa said, "Oh, he chases me all the time. Come Annie, climb up on the table, beside me. Have you ever seen such food?"

"Never!" gasped Annie, shaking with fright.

There were dainty bits of spice cake, and fine cheese, and even a drop of wine in the glasses.

"OOoooh! I am seeing things," squeaked Annie suddenly. "I see a cat!"

"It *is* a cat!" cried Melissa. "Run! Run!"

They slammed the living-room door, just in time.

"Oh!" sobbed Annie. "I have never been so frightened!"

"Nonsense, you'll get used to it," said Melissa. "There, I've put on the music machine. Would you care to dance?"

"No thank you," said Annie and she started to run.

"Annie, where are you going?" called Melissa.

"Home, to the country," squeaked Annie. "Goodbye, Melissa. Thank you for the very nice time. Oh. Help! Oh! Oh! Oh!"

The little mouse ran through the city. She ran and ran and ran. And she did not stop until she was safe in the quiet green country.

That night she told her gentle friends, "I would rather lead a simple life in peace, than dine on riches and live in fear."

# MUSIC MAKING

The conductor leads the orchestra
by waving his baton. The musicians
are playing a very gay tune.
Which of the musical instruments do
you think you could learn to play?

bassoon

double bass

cello

oboe

clarinet

piccolo

baton

violin

flute

piano

conductor

248

podium

cymbals

triangle

snare drum

bass drum

French horn

trumpet

tuba

tambourine

cornet

trombone

guitar

harp

harmonica

comb and
tissue paper

# Trains

This locomotive is called "Puffing Billy." It was made in England.

The "Dewitt Clinton" was an early American train.

The "Lafayette" was another early American locomotive.

Later on, this type of locomotive helped to settle the American West.

This was the first locomotive to have six sets of driving wheels.

Oldtime trains were very gaily painted.

The docksider is used on the docks of a busy port.

The Diesel switcher is used to switch cars in railroad yards.

Modern steam locomotives are being replaced by Diesel and electric engines.

This is a European steam engine pulling a small goods wagon.

Notice the bumpers on these trains.
This is a Diesel engine pulling a tank wagon.

The engine on a rack railway has a toothed wheel which fits into a toothed rail. This is how it pulls itself up steep mountains.

252

The Diesel locomotive is used to pull either freight or passenger trains.

The electric locomotive is used
around big cities and where there
are long tunnels, as it gives off no smoke.

This passenger car has its own motor and is used for short runs.

This electric locomotive gets its power from the wire overhead.

# MORE TRAINS

rear

Annie Ant is walking forward.

front

Father Cat

Dingo ahead

behind

Haggis

Pa Pig

Driver

under

Squeaky

The driver is at the front of the bus. Haggis Dog is at the back of the bus. Annie Ant is walking forward to the front of the bus. Pa Pig is sitting backwards, facing the rear of the bus. Father Cat is behind the bus. Who is ahead of the bus? Who is under it?

Diesel passenger train

gondola car with brakeman's cab

signal

What is Dingo trying to do? Does he think he is a train? Get off those railroad tracks at once, Dingo!

tracks

# Everyone is hurrying to the railroad station to catch a train.

freight station

railroad station

water tank

yard engine

platform

station master

box car

tank car

coal car

bumper

Diesel switcher

steam locomotive

coach car

electric locomotive

engineer

Diesel locomotive

Dingo

signal tower

# Polite Puppy

POLITE PUPPY SAYS,
"BOW WOW, HOW DO YOU DO?"
WHEN HE MEETS SOMEONE.

HE OPENS DOORS
FOR LADIES.

HE SAYS,
"BOW WOW, THANK YOU",
WHEN HE IS GIVEN SOMETHING.

HE SAYS," BOW WOW, PLEASE,"
**WHEN** HE ASKS
FOR SOMETHING.
**AND** - WHEN HE EATS
HIS MEALS, HE.........

.... OH! THAT NAUGHTY PUPPY!
HE HAS FORGOTTEN
HIS MANNERS!
YOU DON'T SIT IN YOUR DISH!
WHEN YOU EAT YOUR MEALS!
DO YOU?

# THE DOG AND HIS BONE

*told by*
*Patricia Scarry*

A little dog hurried to the stream with a large juicy bone in his mouth. He wanted to eat the bone all by himself. So he ran across a log that bridged the stream.

Then, in the water, he saw a picture of himself. But he thought it was another dog.

"Ah, now I shall have two nice bones to eat," thought the greedy little dog.

He growled, and snapped at the other bone.

SPLASH! His bone fell in the water. And so did he! Now he had nothing to eat.

Greedy-greedy makes a hungry puppy!

# THE ALWAYS HUNGRY VISITORS

Mother Cat bought food at the grocery store. She brought it home and put it on the kitchen table.

Look behind you, Mother Cat! You have some hungry visitors.

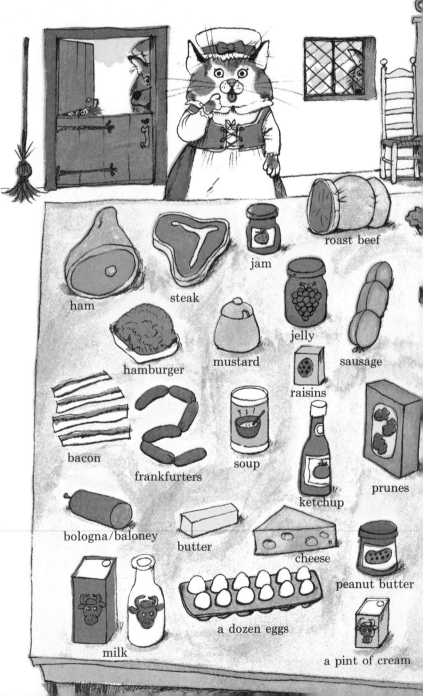

ham

steak

jam

roast beef

hamburger

mustard

jelly

sausage

raisins

bacon

frankfurters

soup

ketchup

prunes

bologna/baloney

butter

cheese

peanut butter

milk

a dozen eggs

a pint of cream

pie

ice
cream

cake

cereal

buns

spaghetti

cocoa

salt

cookies

Mother Cat gave the visitors
a jar of jam to eat.
Where did they ever learn
their table manners?

After they had eaten
they all took naps.

ZZZZZZZZZZ

259

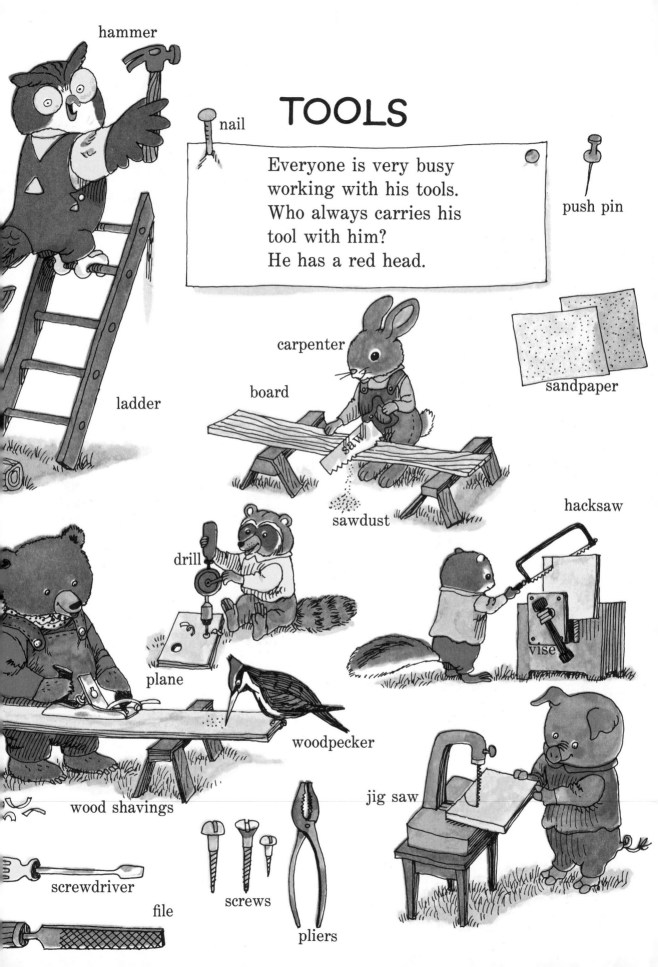

hammer

nail

# TOOLS

Everyone is very busy
working with his tools.
Who always carries his
tool with him?
He has a red head.

push pin

carpenter

board

sandpaper

ladder

saw

sawdust

hacksaw

drill

vise

plane

woodpecker

jig saw

wood shavings

screwdriver

screws

file

pliers

bucksaw

trowel

brick-layer

brick wall

brick

lumber

fence painter

paint brush

ball of twine

saw horse

paint

barrel

tack

tack hammer

ruler

folding ruler

jackknife

tool box

putty knife

shovel

bolt

nut

dirt

compass

wheelbarrow

pickax

# More Mother Goose Rhymes

Little maid, pretty maid, whither goest thou?
Down in the meadow to milk my cow.
Shall I go with thee? No, not now;
When I send for thee, then come thou.

As I was going to St. Ives,
I met a man with seven wives.
Each wife had seven sacks,
Each sack had seven cats,
Each cat had seven kits;
Kits, cats, sacks, and wives,
How many were there
going to St. Ives?

Jack Sprat could eat no fat,
His wife could eat no lean,
And so between them both,
       you see,
They licked the platter clean.

# TREES

twig

branch

leaf

leaves

stem

apple

tree trunk

Some **trees** bear fruit which is good to eat.
MacIntosh Dog is shaking apples out of the apple **tree**.
Be careful you do not shake anything else out, MacIntosh!

hatchet

ax

bow saw

Chips is chopping down
a **tree**. I hope he gets out
of the way before it falls on him!

woods

saw

board

roots

Trees grow in the woods.
Trees are made of wood.
Chips chopped down the tree.
He is sawing it into boards.

chair

ax

stump

log

branch

Chips is sawing the thick branch.

jackknife

saw

Mr. Fixit is sawing the thin branch.
I wonder who will be the first to finish?

# EGG IN THE HOLE

One day, up in the hayloft of the barn, Henny laid an egg.
The egg rolled through a hole in the floor to a room down below.
"Oh my! I hope I haven't lost it!" she said.

   Henny rushed down the stairs to the room below.

   "Have you seen my egg?" asked Henny.

   "Yes, I have," said Billy Goat. "It fell on my ice cream.
Then it rolled along the table and went out the window."

   Henny hurried to the window.

"Have you seen my egg?" she asked.

"Yes, I have," said Little Bird.

"It rolled along the rain gutter and then went down the hole."

Henny ran outside where Pig was sitting.

"Have you seen my egg?" asked Henny. "I'm afraid I have lost it."

"Your egg just hit me on the head," said Pig. "It rolled down my back, through my curly tail, and across the barnyard."

Henny rushed across the barnyard.

She saw her egg just before it rolled into a hole in the ground.

Just then from out of the hole appeared a tiny mouse.

"Henny," he said, "I have found your egg! Something very special happened . . . It is broken and it is in a lot of little pieces! BUT . . .
if you look closely . . .

You will see that you have a brand-new Baby Chick in its place!"

Henny was so pleased! She had lost her egg, but now she had a baby chick instead.

You would be too, wouldn't you?

"Hi, Mommy," said Baby Chick.

268

# SCHTOOMPAH,
## THE FUNNY AUSTRIAN

Schtoompah was a funny fellow. He was not very tidy. Instead of putting things away neatly, he would just throw things in a closet.

He threw his tuba in the closet.

He threw mittens and jackets and rakes into that closet.

He even threw the kitchen stove in by mistake.

And then when he went to look for something he could never find it.

Schtoompah was going to play his tuba for the Saturday night band concert. He spent two whole days looking for his tuba before he finally found it.

Now, he was ready to go to the band concert.

269

Schtoompah put his tuba on his head, and rode his bicycle backwards.

"Oh that Schtoompah, he is a funny fellow," the townspeople all said. "I wonder what funny thing he will do at the band concert?"

The band concert was about to begin.
"Uh-ein, uh-zwei, uh-drei," said the band leader.

Schtoompah blew, but
no music came out.

He blew even harder, but
still no music came out.

Schtoompah took a deep breath;
and blew with all his might. . . .

BLAZZZZZZZZZZZ!

"Oh, that Schtoompah!
He is a funny fellow,"
the townspeople all laughed.

# MERRY MONTHS OF THE YEAR

*by Patricia Scarry*

# JANUARY

**January** starts the brand-new year with snow for sledding, skiing, snowmen. There are icy ponds for skating on.

Mittens drip,
And there's cocoa to sip.
This month there's a nice thing to do:
Throw crumbs to the birds! They're hungry too.

# F·E·B·R·U·A·R·Y

**February** is slushy and short. Only 28 days to play,
Some of them sunny, most of them gray.
Then every four years there is Leap Year, with 29 days.
The best one of all is Valentine's Day.

# M·A·R·C·H

**March** is gusty, muddy, blustery. This is the month for flying kites, roller-skating, rattly nights.

Wear something green on St. Patrick's Day.

Robins sing, "Spring is on the way!"

And bears wake up from their winter's sleep.

# A·P·R·I·L

**April** is fun! The very first day is April Fool's,
a day for playing jokes.

All month long the weather teases.

Now it's warm, then, oops! the sneezes!

Take off your boots and it will shower:

Then the sun shines for an hour.

Robins are nesting, puddles are skiddy, violets pop!

No wonder April's gay and funny—

You know who's coming? The Easter Bunny!

# MAY

May—and it's time to play outdoors again.
The world is filled with flowers.
    On lawns and hills and window sills
    Are sunny, saucy daffodils!
    And everywhere I hear the sound of little things
    Bravely trying out new wings.
    Ducks are quacky, turtles snappy.
    I think my heart will not be still
    'til I roll down a grassy hill.

# JUNE

**June**—and school is over soon!
  Then all we'll do each day
  Is play and play—hooray!
  Summer arrives June 21st—the longest day of the year.
  We'll laze on the grass and listen, and hear:
  Bees buzzing! Hummingbirds whirring! Worms wiggling!
  June is laughing, golden, giggling!
  Today I'll visit the brook and dip in my toes.
  I'll perch at the edge, and hope a butterfly lands on
      my nose.

# JULY

**July** begins with a *boom!*
    Sometimes it's thunder,
    With lightning in the sky.
    Sometimes it's the rummy-tum-tum
    Of a drummer marching by.
You can get dressed up and carry flags,
And play in your very own band.
And now is the time to make cold drinks
To sell at your lemonade stand.
    At night, if you see a star fall, *swiiish!*
    Be sure to make a lovely wish.

**August** is steamy, hot, ice-creamy.
   Maybe you'll visit the seashore . . .
   Play under the garden hose . . .
   Swing in the hammock with bare toes.
Summer is nearly over, and birds stay up late.
Suppers are hot-dogs, cooked out of doors—
   So good you can hardly wait!

# SEPTEMBER

**September** is new shoes, and back to school.
Grapes are plumping, apples turn red.
Nuts are browning. It's early to bed.
Squirrels are storing their nuts away.
Days are short; there's less time to play.
Autumn's here. The summer's gone.
Better put your sweater on.

# OCTOBER

**October** is orange and red and brown.
See the leaves all tumble down!
  Rake them up into piles so high
  You can jump in them, and flop, and lie.
Now the farmer harvests his hay.
The barn is filled. And every day is growing shorter.
We have to wait the whole long month for
  spooky Hallowe'en.
What are you going to be? A ghost? A witch?
  Or a queen?

# NOVEMBER

**November** smells of turkey, grapes, and pumpkin pie,
And leaf-smoke curling gently into the sky.
  Some animals have burrowed into the earth
  To sleep until the spring.
  Is a cricket sharing your house for the winter?
  Can you hear him sing?
Nature's garden is resting.
  The trees are stark and bare.
  Now you can see the lovely nests
  You didn't know were there.

# DECEMBER

**December** is waiting and wanting and wishing
and longing for Christmas Day.
This is the merriest month of all—
Make a cranberry rope, a popcorn ball,
Cookies to hang on the tree,
Hide presents in places where none can see.
We try to be as good as gold all month, so very good,
because we know who's coming down the chimney—
Jolly Santa Claus!

# More Mother Goose Rhymes

I see the moon, and the moon sees me.
God bless the moon, and God bless me.

Star light, star bright,
First star I see tonight,
I wish I may, I wish I might,
Have the wish I wish tonight.

Twinkle, twinkle, little star,
How I wonder what you are!
Up above the world so high,
Like a diamond in the sky.

When the blazing sun is gone,
When he nothing shines upon,
Then you show your little light,
Twinkle, twinkle, all the night.

Good night,
Sleep tight,
Wake up bright
In the morning light,
To do what's right
With all your might.

LOOK! Who is that riding home on his bicycle?
WHY! It is Schtoompah!
He has drawn a funny face on his tuba.
My, he is a funny fellow!
I hope he remembers to put his tuba away
neatly, in his closet, don't you?
Do you ever forget to put your tuba away
in your closet, before you go to bed?
Do you?

THE END